The Trouble with Magic

by RUTH CHEW

Illustrated by the author

SCHOLASTIC INC.

New York Toronto London Auckland Sydney Tokyo

ISBN: 0-590-10343-1

Readability level is determined by using the Spache Readability Formula. 2.2 signifies high 2nd-grade level.

12 11 10 9 8 7 6 5 4 3 2 1   4   5 6 7 8 9/8 0/9

Printed in the U.S.A.   28

To the memory of
Rick Foels

1

"Pew!" Barbara ran out onto the front porch.

Her brother came out of the house after her. He slammed the door behind him. "If *you* won't tell Mrs. Cunningham to stop cooking cabbage, Barb, I will."

"Don't you dare, Rick Benton! Mother told us to be good to Mrs. Cunningham. She's such a nice old lady. Remember the woman who took care of us the last time Mother and Daddy were away."

Rick made a face. "Miss Henry wouldn't ever let us go anywhere. She made us stay in the house all the time or else play on the front walk."

"Mrs. Cunningham even gave us a front door key," Barbara said. She sat down on the porch steps. "Oh, I wish she didn't like cabbage. It smells so awful."

Rick scratched his head. "Hey, Barb, I've got an idea. Do you have any money?"

"I still have my allowance from last week." Barbara took two quarters out of the pocket of her jacket.

"Come on, then. We can buy a spray can to get rid of the cabbage smell." Rick started down the steps.

Barbara stood up. She wanted to save the quarters to buy a birthday present for her mother. But, "First things first." That's what her mother always said.

Barbara followed Rick down the Brooklyn street. The maple trees were clouded over with pale green blossoms. The children walked to the supermarket on Church Avenue.

Rick found a shelf stacked with spray cans. He read the labels. "Do we want the house to smell like a tropic garden or a South Sea isle?"

Barbara looked at the price. "Sixty-nine cents."

Rick took a green bottle down from the shelf. "These are cheaper than the cans. There's a wick in them that you pull up. This one is marked down. It only costs a quarter."

"Maybe there's something wrong with it." Barbara looked at the bottle. The cap was rusty, and the label was blurred. Otherwise it seemed to be all right.

After Barbara paid for the bottle at the checkout counter, the two children went out of the supermarket. "It's raining," Rick said.

"Come on, then. I've got to get started with my homework," Barbara told him. "We can open the bottle and put it in my room for a while."

"What about my room?" Rick asked.

"I paid for the bottle," Barbara said. "And I always have more homework than you do. You can borrow the bottle later."

The rain was coming down harder. Rick and Barbara began to run. By the time they got home it was pouring. Mrs. Cunningham opened the front door. "I thought I heard you come in before, children. You're late getting home from school. Give me those wet jackets."

Barbara took off her jacket. "We did come home before, Mrs. Cunningham. We had to go to the store for something."

"Would you like some milk and cookies?" Mrs. Cunningham asked.

"Yes," Rick said. "But not right now." He handed her his jacket. "We have to do something first." He ran up the stairs with the bottle and took it to Barbara's room.

Barbara came in after him and shut the door.

Rick was struggling to get the cap off the bottle. "It's stuck."

"Give it to me." Barbara tried turning the bottle cap. She was two years older than Rick. Her hands were stronger. But she couldn't open the bottle either.

Barbara took a metal paperweight off the top of her desk. She used it to bang the edges of the bottle cap. Still the cap wouldn't budge.

"I've got a pair of pliers in my room." Rick ran to get them.

Barbara fitted the pliers on the bottle cap and twisted. Now the cap turned. She lifted it off and stuck her thumb and forefinger into the bottle.

Suddenly Barbara felt cold all over. "Rick!" she whispered. "Something has hold of my fingers!"

2

BARBARA was shaking so much she could hardly pull her hand out of the bottle. Something small and black clung to the end of her finger.

As soon as Barbara's hand was out of the bottle the black thing began to grow. At first Rick and Barbara couldn't tell what it was. Then they saw it was a man. He was wearing a black suit and holding a black umbrella over his head. The man got bigger and bigger and bigger until he blocked the light from the window. The room was getting dark. In a minute Barbara and Rick would be squashed.

"Stop!" Barbara cried.

At once the huge shape began to shrink. It got smaller and smaller. Then it stopped.

The man closed the umbrella. "How do you like this size?"

Barbara was still shaking. She opened her mouth, but she couldn't say a word.

Rick swallowed. "It's a nice size," he said. "You're just about as big as the man who runs the bakery on Church Avenue."

Barbara stared at the little man. He

was short and tubby. His eyes were bright blue in a round pink face. When he took off his tall, wide-brimmed black hat, Barbara saw that the top of his head was bald. He had a ring of gray curls around the back and curly gray sideburns. His black suit seemed a little too tight for him.

Suddenly Barbara wasn't afraid any more. "Are you a genie?" she asked.

The little man's face became even pinker. "Oh my goodness, no." He smiled shyly. "I'm a wizard. My name is Harrison Peabody, but you can call me Harry." He gave a little bow. "What's your name?"

"I'm Barbara Benton. This is my brother, Rick."

"If you're not a genie," Rick said, "what were you doing in the bottle?"

Harrison Peabody coughed. His face turned bright red. For a minute he didn't answer. Then he said, "It's a long story. I went into the bottle just for a minute.

And then some busybody came along and put the top on. And I couldn't get out."

"If you're a wizard," Barbara said, "you ought to know enough magic to get out of a bottle."

Harrison Peabody lowered his voice. "Bottles," he said, "are very bad for magic. Don't ever go into one."

"I won't," Barbara promised. Then she said, "Why did you grab my fingers?"

"I wanted to be sure I got out of the bottle before you put the cap back on. Once before somebody opened that bottle to smell it and then shut it so fast I got banged on the head."

Rick looked into the bottle. "No wick," he said. "We wasted a quarter."

"What do you mean?" Harrison Peabody asked.

"Barbara bought the bottle to get rid of the awful smell around here," Rick told him.

The little man sniffed the air. "It smells good to me."

"What did you eat when you were in the bottle?" Barbara asked.

"There was nothing to eat but the wick," the wizard said. "I used to bite off little bits and pretend it was different things. One time I'd make believe it was roast beef. Another time it would be ice cream. Yesterday I finished the last piece. It really wasn't bad."

"Well, I guess Rick and I are stuck with the smell of cabbage," Barbara said.

"What kind of smell would you like?" Harrison Peabody asked.

"Roses." Barbara put the cap back on the bottle.

The little wizard walked to the window and looked out. It was raining hard. "Roses, please," he said, and opened the umbrella.

3

Little pink roses began to grow out of the lamp on Barbara's desk. She bent over to sniff them. "They're real! How lovely, Harry." Barbara turned to look at the wizard.

Harrison Peabody was dancing around the room, holding the black umbrella over his head. A climbing rose covered with bright red blooms crawled up one wall. "I haven't had so much fun in a long time. You've no idea how boring it was in that bottle."

Suddenly Barbara saw that there were roses everywhere. They grew from under the bed, twined around the mirror, and crowded out of the dresser drawers. "Stop!" Barbara said.

The wizard stopped dancing. He closed the umbrella. "What's the matter? I thought you liked roses?" The little man looked sad.

Barbara didn't want to hurt his feelings. "I do, Harry." She stood on tiptoe to sniff a huge white rose that hung down from the light fixture. "They're lovely. Thank you."

Rick was feeling the petals of a yellow rose. "You're terrific, Harry."

The wizard beamed.

"It's late," Barbara said. "I'd better go get the cookies. Mrs. Cunningham doesn't like us to eat right before supper. Do you want some, Harry?"

"Yes, please," the little man said.

Barbara wondered how long he'd been shut up in the bottle, nibbling on the wick. She ran downstairs.

Rick called after her. "Don't forget me."

Mrs. Cunningham was in the kitchen peeling apples. She looked up when Barbara came into the room. "The cookies are in the cookie jar in the dining room, dear. Get yourself a glass of milk."

Barbara took a container of milk out of the refrigerator. "I'll take some up to Rick." She pulled three paper cups from the dispenser in the kitchen and went to load her pockets with cookies.

When Barbara got to the top of the stairs, she found Rick and the wizard waiting for her. They both had big grins on their faces. Barbara was sure they had been up to something, but she pretended not to be interested. She filled the paper cups with milk and divided the cookies into three parts. Barbara took her milk and cookies into her room and sat down at her desk to do her homework.

4

BARBARA was trying to read her social studies book. The roses on the lamp cast dark shadows on the page. She twisted her chair to get in a better light. "Ouch!" Her leg had touched a thorny vine that poked out of the kneehole of her desk. Barbara tried to move it out of the way. A thorn stabbed her finger.

Barbara sucked her finger for a minute. Then she went to look for Harrison Peabody.

Rick had gone downstairs to put the milk container back in the refrigerator. The wizard was sitting on the top step finishing his last cookie. He looked up at Barbara and smiled. "Delicious!" He licked the crumbs from his fingers.

"Harry," Barbara said, "please would you take away some of the roses. There are too many. I don't have room to work at my desk."

The little man got to his feet and picked up the umbrella. He followed Barbara into her room. It had stopped raining. The late afternoon sun was shining through the window. It brought out all the different colors of the roses. They looked even more beautiful than before.

The wizard rubbed his chin. "Wonderful job, even if I say it myself. It seems a shame to spoil it."

"I know," Barbara said. "But I have

such a lot of homework. And I can't even get started."

"Couldn't you do your homework somewhere else?" Harrison Peabody asked.

"If I did it downstairs, Mrs. Cunningham would want to know why. She knows I have my own desk," Barbara said. "She might even look into this room. What would I tell her if she saw all the roses?"

"Don't you have a key to your room? You could lock it up," the wizard suggested.

Barbara looked around the room. She wondered if the roses would have to be watered. That would be pretty messy. "Harry," she said, "maybe you ought to take away all the roses."

"But the room would smell like cabbage again," the little man reminded her.

Barbara had a feeling that he was stalling. She looked him straight in the face. "I know I said I wanted the room to smell like roses. But I never meant anything like this. Please will you take them away?"

"Magic," Harrison Peabody said, "is easier to do than to undo."

"You mean you *can't* take the roses away?" Barbara said.

The little man wouldn't look at Barbara. Instead he gazed out of the window at the bright sunshine. "Well," he said, "not right now."

At this moment Rick came into the room. His eyes were shining. "Hey, Barb, come with me. I've got something to show you."

Barbara picked up her school books. She took a notebook and pencil off the top of her desk. Maybe Rick would let her use his room to study. He never spent much time on his homework.

Rick grabbed Barbara's hand and

pulled her down the hall to his room. He looked at her and grinned. "Open the door, Barb."

Barbara turned the handle, and the door swung open. It was very dark in the room. Barbara felt for the light switch. She touched something rough and hard like the bark of a tree. Barbara peered into the gloom. As her eyes became used to the shadows she saw that there was a fat tree growing out of the floor between Rick's bed and his dresser. The branches stretched right across the room. One of them was jammed against the light switch. Smaller trees were growing around Rick's desk. Underfoot there was a thick carpet of pine needles.

For a minute Barbara just stood in the doorway. Then she said, "I suppose you told Harry you wanted your room to smell like a pine woods."

Rick nodded. "How did you guess?"

5

BARBARA lay on her stomach on the tile floor of the bathroom. She propped her social studies book against one of the legs of the sink and spread her notebook open in front of her. It wasn't as easy as working at her desk. But there was plenty of light for reading. And by the time someone banged on the door Barbara had finished most of her homework.

"Who is it?" Barbara asked.

"Me," Rick said. "Mrs. Cunningham is calling us to come to supper."

"Where's Harry?" Barbara wanted to know.

"In my room," Rick said. "Why?"

Barbara got up off the floor. "We have to take him something to eat. He's only had cookies and milk. I think he's hungry. And we ought to find a place where he can sleep. There isn't room for both of you in your bed."

"Oh, he says he'll be leaving soon," Rick told her.

"We can't let him go," Barbara whispered. "He has to unmagic those rooms. They can't stay the way they are."

"Of course," Rick said. "I've been having fun in my room, but Harry has a bush growing out of my pillow. I'd have trouble sleeping in the bed. We can tell him to change the rooms back before he goes."

"Didn't he tell you?" Barbara said. "He says he *can't* change the rooms back now. I don't know if he's forgotten how. Anyway, we'll have to keep him here until he does change them."

They heard Mrs. Cunningham's voice. "Barbara, Rick, come along. Supper will get cold."

"Go downstairs," Barbara said to her brother. "Tell Mrs. Cunningham I'm coming."

She ran down the hall to Rick's room and opened the door. Harrison Peabody was sitting on the low branch of a tree. He was swinging his legs and gazing through the pine boughs out of the window.

"Harry," Barbara said in a low voice, "just wait here. We'll bring you some supper."

6

Mrs. Cunningham had made stuffed cabbage for supper. Neither Rick nor Barbara had ever tasted it before. Barbara was about to eat her second helping when she remembered the wizard. She poked Rick under the table. "Save some for Harry," she whispered.

Barbara looked around for something to put the stuffed cabbage in. She had not yet poured any milk into her glass. When Mrs. Cunningham went into the kitchen to take the pie out of the oven, Barbara filled the glass with stuffed cabbage. She wedged it between her knees under the tablecloth.

Rick crammed a load of cabbage into the butter dish. He fitted the lid over it.

When Mrs. Cunningham came back from the kitchen she saw the children's empty plates. She smiled. "Who would like some hot apple pie?"

Harrison Peabody picnicked under the trees in Rick's room. They still hadn't figured out how to get to the light switch. But Rick had a flashlight that his father had given him. It gave just enough light for the wizard to see his supper. He sat cross-legged on the pine needles. Rick and Barbara sat one on each side of him and watched him eat.

He liked the stuffed cabbage just as much as the children had. The little man said the apple pie was the best he'd ever eaten. He didn't at all mind eating it out of a sugar bowl. "I never had any silverware in the bottle either," he told them.

When supper was over Barbara said, "I've been thinking, Harry. You could live in our attic. There's a mattress up there for you to sleep on. And Rick and I could take food up to you."

"I didn't see any attic stairs," the wizard said.

"There aren't any stairs." Rick opened the door of his room and pointed to a trapdoor on the hall ceiling near the bathroom. "You have to use a stepladder. We've got one in the basement. I'll go get it."

Rick went downstairs. Mrs. Cunningham had finished the dishes. She was sitting in the living room watching television. When Rick came up from the basement with the stepladder, he had to walk past the living room to get to the stairs.

"What do you want the ladder for, Rick?" Mrs. Cunningham asked.

"I have to put something in the attic," Rick said.

"Well, bring the ladder right down when you've finished with it, dear," Mrs. Cunningham said. "I know your mother wouldn't want it cluttering the upstairs hall."

Rick took the ladder upstairs. He set it up in the hall under the trapdoor. The little wizard waited while Barbara climbed up and pushed the trapdoor open. She stood on the top step and looked into the attic. "It's awfully dark in there, Rick. You'd better lend Harry your flashlight."

"What will I use in my room?" Rick asked. "It's dark too."

Barbara thought for a moment. "Mother has a little flashlight on her night table," she said. "Harry could use that."

Rick got his mother's flashlight. He handed it up to Barbara. She climbed into the attic and beamed the light all around.

The attic ceiling was low and slanting.

Barbara saw the mattress rolled up in a corner. A chest of clothes stood against a wall. Next to it were three cardboard boxes full of files from her father's office. There was a baby carriage covered with a plastic dropcloth, a broken television set, a pile of dusty phonograph records, and stacks and stacks of old magazines. Everywhere she looked there were spiderwebs. The one window of the attic was covered with them. When a fat gray mouse scurried across the floor Barbara almost dropped the flashlight.

Rick held the ladder steady while Harrison Peabody climbed up. The tubby little wizard scrambled into the attic.

The two children cleared a space on the floor. They unrolled the mattress on it.

"I'm afraid it's not very fancy," Barbara told the wizard.

"It's much better than living in a bottle," Harrison Peabody said.

7

"How are we going to get food to you, Harry?" Rick asked. "Mrs. Cunningham told me not to leave the ladder upstairs."

"Don't you have a rope?" the wizard wanted to know.

"There's some clothesline in the basement," Barbara said. She handed the flashlight to the little man and backed out of the attic onto the stepladder. Rick followed her. Harrison Peabody closed the trapdoor.

"Take the stepladder down if you're going to the basement, Barb," Rick said. "I'd better get busy with my homework."

"There's a good light in the bathroom," Barbara told him. She picked up the aluminum stepladder and carried it down to the basement.

The clothesline was on top of the washing machine. There was a broom beside the freezer. Barbara decided to take the broom upstairs too.

Mrs. Cunningham was watching an old Greta Garbo movie on television. She never even looked up when Barbara passed the living room door.

Barbara tied the clothesline to the end of the broom. She stood on tiptoe to tap the trapdoor with the broom handle. There was no answer. Barbara tapped again.

This time the trapdoor moved a very little bit. Harrison Peabody peeked through the crack beside the door.

"Harry," Barbara whispered, "here's your rope."

The trapdoor opened a little wider. The wizard untied the clothesline from the broom handle and pulled it up into the attic. Now it was his turn to whisper. "Barbara, do you have a pair of scissors?"

"I'll get some." Barbara took the broom to her bedroom. She propped it between her bed and a large bush covered with yellow roses. Then she went downstairs to get the scissors from her mother's sewing cabinet.

When she came back with them, Harrison Peabody lowered the clothesline into the hall. "Tie the scissors to the end of this," he said. Barbara tied the scissors to the clothesline. The wizard pulled them up into the attic and closed the trapdoor.

Mrs. Cunningham called, "Rick, it's your bedtime."

Barbara could hear her starting up the stairs. "Rick's in the bathroom already, Mrs. Cunningham," she yelled. Barbara ran to the end of the hall to make sure Rick's door was closed. Then she rushed back to meet Mrs. Cunningham.

Mrs. Cunningham was carrying a tray with two glasses of milk on it. She walked over to Barbara's door. Barbara got to her before she could put her hand on the knob. "Let me help you, Mrs. Cunningham. I'll give Rick his milk."

"You're a sweet child. Thank you." Mrs. Cunningham handed the tray to Barbara and walked across the hall to her own room.

8

WHEN Barbara heard Rick come out of the bathroom she gave him the milk. "I was afraid to put it in your room," she said. "You'd be sure to knock it over in the dark."

Rick was still dressed. "Take your shower first, Barb. I've got to go look for my pyjamas in that pine forest." He went down the hall to his room.

Barbara rushed to get ready for bed. She waited until Rick had finished washing and was in his room with the door closed. Then she knocked on Mrs. Cunningham's door. "The bathroom's clear. Good night. See you in the morning."

"Good night, dear," Mrs. Cunningham said.

Barbara went to sleep with the sweet smell of roses all around her. Sometime in the night she was awakened by a light shining in her face. She opened her eyes.

Rick was standing beside her bed with his flashlight in his hand. "I can't sleep with that bush in my bed," he said.

Barbara sat up in bed. "It's chilly," she said. "And we forgot to give Harry a blanket." Barbara got up, taking care not to scratch her feet on the roses sticking out from under her bed. She put on her bathrobe and slippers and went with Rick to get a blanket from the linen closet in the bathroom.

It was dark in the hall. But there was a light coming from under the bathroom door. Barbara tried the knob. The door was locked. Then something brushed against her face. Barbara grabbed Rick.

He clicked on the flashlight.

"Look!" Rick pointed to the ceiling.

The trapdoor was open. A rope ladder dangled from it almost to the floor. The ladder had swung against Barbara's face.

"That's our clothesline!" she whispered. "The wizard cut it up to make a rope ladder. And we'll be blamed for it."

"I guess Harry is too fat to shinny up a rope," Rick said. "Anyway, it's a neat ladder."

There was the sound of water splashing in the bathroom.

"Harry must be taking a shower." Rick started to climb up the rope ladder. Barbara came up after him.

The wizard had folded his clothes in a neat pile on the mattress. Right on top were the black hat and the black umbrella. Barbara looked at the umbrella. She was sure it was what the wizard used to do his magic.

She picked up the umbrella and opened it.

"You'd better not mess with the wizard's things," Rick warned her.

All at once there was a crash of thunder.

Both children jumped. Now they could hear the rain. It was beating against the attic window.

Rick ran to the trapdoor. "Let's get out of here, Barb." He started to climb back down the rope ladder.

Barbara looked up at the umbrella. She might never get another chance. "Could you please take away the roses and the pine trees and make our rooms the way they were?" she begged.

The umbrella seemed to quiver in her hand.

Barbara closed it. She laid it back on top of the pile of clothes on the mattress.

9

BARBARA climbed down the rope ladder after Rick. She had just stepped off it onto the floor of the hall when the bathroom door opened. Harrison Peabody came out. Barbara held her breath. Suppose by some magic the wizard knew she'd been playing with his umbrella!

He was wearing a red velvet evening coat. Barbara remembered that her mother had packed it away in the attic. The little man's gray curls were damp. And his face was even pinker than usual. Rick could smell his father's after-shave lotion.

"What should I do with these?" Harrison Peabody asked. He handed his socks and his underwear to Barbara. "I washed them out, but I didn't think I should leave them in the bathroom. And there's no good place to hang them in the attic."

Rick took a blanket and a pillow out of the linen closet in the bathroom. He gave them to the wizard. "Go to bed, Harry," Rick whispered. "And please *stay* there. Mrs. Cunningham will have a fit if she sees you."

Harrison Peabody tucked the pillow and blanket under one arm. He wrapped the red velvet coat tightly around his tubby little form and climbed the rope ladder into the attic. Then he pulled up the ladder and closed the trapdoor.

Rick went back to his room.

Barbara looked at the damp socks and underwear. I guess I can hang them on a rose bush, she told herself.

But when Barbara opened the door of her bedroom there wasn't a rose to be seen. She hung the socks and the underwear over a chair near the radiator and went back to bed.

10

BARBARA and Rick were both late getting up next morning. Mrs. Cunningham had to call Rick three times. The children rushed to get ready for school.

It was still raining. Mrs. Cunningham insisted that they wear raincoats and rubbers. Rick had forgotten that his rubbers were under the refrigerator in the back pantry. By the time he found them it was almost eight-thirty.

They were splashing through the puddles toward school.

"I slept O.K. after you fixed my room, Barb," Rick said. "I wonder why Harry wouldn't do it."

"Yipe!" Barbara said. "Harry's underwear and socks are still in my room. Suppose Mrs. Cunningham finds them!"

"And we forgot to take him any breakfast," Rick said. "He might go down to the kitchen to get something to eat."

The two children turned around and began to run home. When they reached the house they raced up the front steps. Rick pushed the doorbell. There was no answer. He pushed it again. "Mrs. Cunningham must have gone to the supermarket."

Barbara remembered her door key. She fished it out of her pocket and opened the front door. Then she ran upstairs. She saw the broom on her bedroom floor.

Barbara picked it up and took the socks and underwear off the back of her desk chair.

Rick hurried to the kitchen for a box of cornflakes and a container of milk. He took a bowl and a spoon and went upstairs.

Barbara was standing in the hall under the trapdoor waiting for him. She banged with the broom handle on the trapdoor of the attic. "Harry, open up!"

The trapdoor opened. Harrison Peabody looked down. "Good morning." He dropped one end of the ladder through the opening.

Rick climbed up. "We brought you some breakfast."

"Thank you, but I've already had some," the wizard said.

Rick pulled himself into the attic. Barbara followed him. The children blinked their eyes.

"How do you like it?" Harrison Peabody asked. He looked very pleased with himself.

The whole attic was changed. Not a cobweb was left. The dusty records and magazines were gone. There was no sign of the baby carriage or the boxes of files. Lace curtains fluttered in the little arched window. A pretty fringed rug was in the middle of the shiny dark floor. And on the rug stood a table and four chairs.

The table was set with a white cloth and blue dishes. The children saw a platter of crunchy little sausages. Hot cocoa steamed in a big pitcher. And a stack of waffles was ready on a plate beside a jar of honey. Harrison Peabody wore a new black and white checked suit and red socks.

The wizard didn't say anything about changing the children's rooms. Barbara began to wonder whether it was she or

Harrison Peabody who had unmagicked them.

When the little man saw the socks and underwear Barbara was holding, he took them from her. "Thank you," he said. "Now may I offer you a waffle?"

"They sure smell good," Rick said.

"We'll be late for school," Barbara reminded him.

Rick remembered the last time he was late. "We'll have to go to the school office for late passes."

The wizard picked up the black umbrella. "Maybe I can help you." He opened the umbrella and waved it over the children. "Get them to school on time," he said, "please."

Rick and Barbara looked around. The wizard had disappeared. They were standing in line in the school yard. The last bell was ringing. And it was raining hard.

II

IT STOPPED raining sometime during the morning. And when Rick and Barbara went home for lunch the new little leaves on the hedges were sparkling in the sunlight.

Mrs. Cunningham had made a big pot of vegetable soup. Both children had second helpings. Rick would have liked a third, but there wasn't time. They had to be back at school by one o'clock.

"Harry can magic up something to eat," Rick said. "We don't have to worry about him. Come on, Barb."

They left their rubbers and raincoats at home and walked back to school. At three o'clock Rick waited for Barbara in the school yard. They ran home together.

They were out of breath when they reached the block where their house was. Rick slowed to a walk. "I want to see what Harry is up to. I'll bet he's thought of a lot of magic he can do in the attic."

Barbara was quiet. She was thinking. "What I don't understand," she said, "is why we had to take him food last night."

"Maybe the umbrella doesn't like stuffed cabbage," Rick said.

When they got home Mrs. Cunningham had graham crackers and milk ready for them in the kitchen. "Eat now, children," she said. "If you eat later, you'll spoil your supper." Mrs. Cunningham was stuffing a chicken.

Rick and Barbara finished their after-school snack and raced upstairs. Barbara looked for the broom. She must have left it in the hall this morning. If she asked where it was, Mrs. Cunningham might ask why she wanted it.

Rick had an idea. He told Barbara to hold a chair steady while he stood on the back of it and tapped on the trapdoor with a yardstick.

Rick only had to knock once when the wizard opened the trapdoor. "Did you bring me anything to eat?" Harrison Peabody whispered.

"Let down the ladder, Harry," Barbara whispered back.

The little man lowered the rope ladder. Rick climbed up. Barbara put the chair back in her room. Then she too climbed into the attic.

The sun was shining through the lace curtains. The attic would have looked very nice except that the table was covered with dirty dishes. There were

some cold, greasy-looking sausages left
on the platter. The waffles were limp, and
the cocoa had a skin on it.

"Why didn't you magic away the
mess?" Rick asked the wizard.

"I never had a chance," Harrison Peabody said.

"What do you mean?" Barbara asked.

The little man didn't answer her. He
turned even pinker than he was before
and looked at the floor.

Suddenly Barbara was sorry for him.
"What's the matter, Harry?"

"I've never told anyone before,"

Harrison Peabody said. "You'll laugh at me."

Barbara put her hand on his arm. "No, we won't, Harry."

"I'm not really a powerful wizard," the little man said in a very small voice. "I'm not even a very good one."

"Yes, you are," Rick told him.

Harrison Peabody shook his head. "The only magic I have is in my umbrella. And I have to be very polite to it, or it won't do what I want."

"Now I know why you always say 'please' to it," Barbara said.

"You mean you were rude to the umbrella, and it got mad and wouldn't wash the dishes?" Rick wanted to know.

"No, no, nothing like that," the wizard said.

"Then what happened?" Rick persisted.

"The umbrella," Harrison Peabody explained, "only works when it's raining."

12

AFTER supper Mrs. Cunningham wanted to watch a Rudolph Valentino movie on television.

"I'll load the dishwasher for you," Barbara told her.

Mrs. Cunningham scrubbed the pots and pans and then went into the living room. Rick went down into the basement to look for the broom. He found it in the laundry room.

"Hide it in your room after we use it," Barbara told him. She was putting left-over roast chicken and chocolate pudding into a plastic bag for Rick to take to Harrison Peabody. "He must be starved," Barbara said.

Rick hid the plastic bag under his shirt front. He took the broom and went quietly upstairs. Barbara went on loading the dishwasher.

Barbara had an idea. She took a white garbage bag from the carton on the kitchen shelf and ran upstairs with it.

Rick was in the attic. He had pulled up the rope ladder and was just about to shut the trapdoor when Barbara came down the hall. "Rick!" she called in a low voice.

Her brother looked down at her. Barbara held up the garbage bag. "Let's put Harry's breakfast dishes in this," she said. "I'll stick them in the dishwasher."

Rick let down the ladder for Barbara to climb up. Between them they cleared the table and loaded everything into the garbage bag. Barbara backed carefully down the ladder and took her load downstairs. She stacked the blue dishes in the dishwasher and hid the waffles and sausages under the chicken bones in the kitchen garbage can.

Barbara turned on the dishwasher. While the dishes were washing she went back upstairs. The big pitcher of cold cocoa was still in the attic. Rick and the wizard managed to carry it down the ladder. Barbara dumped the cocoa down

the toilet and washed the pitcher in the bathtub. She dried it with a clean bath towel and took it back to the attic. Then she went to get the blue dishes from the dishwasher.

When Barbara had finished, the attic looked much nicer.

Tomorrow was Saturday. "We can take Harry for a picnic in the park," Rick said.

"We'd better go to bed." Barbara walked to the trapdoor. She took a last look around the attic. It really was a pretty room now.

"Oh, Harry!" Barbara said.

"What's the matter?" the wizard asked.

"You magicked away the mattress," Barbara pointed out.

"So I did," the wizard said.

"What will you sleep on?" Rick asked.

"I'll curl up on the rug." The little man smiled. "And it's still better than living in a bottle."

13

Mrs. Cunningham was packing a picnic lunch. Barbara was helping her. "Do you want one or two baloney sandwiches?" Barbara asked Rick.

"Three," Rick told her. He hoped the wizard liked baloney.

Rick went into the basement for the stepladder. He took it upstairs while Mrs. Cunningham was busy in the kitchen. The wizard would have to use it to get down from the attic. They couldn't leave the trapdoor open with the rope ladder hanging out of it.

Harrison Peabody backed down the stepladder. He was wearing his tall black hat, his new checked suit, and was carrying the black umbrella.

"You won't need the umbrella," Rick said. "It's a lovely day."

"At this time of year," the wizard said, "you never can tell."

Rick put the stepladder behind the door in his room. He went downstairs. Mrs. Cunningham was still in the kitchen with Barbara. Rick gave a low whistle. Harrison Peabody tiptoed down the stairs, and Rick let him out of the front door.

"Wait for us on the sidewalk," Rick told the little man.

Prospect Park is very large. Today it was crowded with people walking their dogs, riding horses on the bridle path, fishing in the lake, or just sitting on the benches in the sunshine.

Rick and Barbara took Harrison Peabody to the top of a hill called Lookout Mountain. From there they could see far out over the trees and houses of Brooklyn. They walked across the Long Meadow and past the boat house and the band shell. At noontime they sat on the rocks near the little stream and ate their lunch. Rick saw a crayfish in the stream. He tried to catch it, but it was too fast for him.

When the sandwiches were all gone and the last drop of lemonade drunk, they put their litter in a trash basket. Then they went to the lake. Barbara saw a flock

of mallard ducks swimming toward the shore. She stood on the stone wall at the edge of the lake. "Look at that funny duck!"

One of the ducks had a much longer neck than the others. It was a different color too. Instead of being brown or having a dark green head, this duck was a pale silvery green all over.

Rick stared at it. "Maybe it's a goose."

Harrison Peabody turned to look at the strange duck. A gust of wind caught his hat and tore it off his head. Rick chased after the hat. Before he could catch it, the hat was blown into the water.

There were rusty cans and broken bottles in the lake. Rick didn't want to go wading. He knelt down on the stone wall and tried to reach the hat, but it drifted away from him.

Barbara saw an old man whose hat had been blown off too. She ran after the hat

and caught it before it went into the lake.
Barbara gave it back to the old man.

"Thank you," he said. "You'd better go
home, little girl. There's going to be a
storm."

Barbara looked at the sky. Dark clouds
covered the sun. Two boys with fishing
poles ran past her. The lake was covered
with choppy waves. All the people in the
park were getting ready to leave.

Harrison Peabody still stood on the stone wall at the edge of the lake. He was looking across the water. Rick went over to him. "Sorry I couldn't get your hat, Harry."

The wizard felt his bald head. "Did I lose it? Well, never mind. It's not the first time."

Barbara remembered the duck. She could still see it swimming through the choppy waves. The water foamed behind it for quite a long time. And now and then something silvery green seemed to loop up into the air out of the foam.

The duck turned to look at them. It dived into the water and came up with something black in its mouth. Then it began to swim in a straight line toward Harrison Peabody.

As it came closer Rick and Barbara saw that it wasn't a duck at all. It had a head like a lizard's. And it was covered with shining scales.

When it reached the stone wall, the creature reared its long neck high up out of the water. It placed the black thing it had in its mouth on the wizard's head.

"Isn't this your hat, Peabody?" a husky voice said. "I'd know it anywhere."

14

ALL the other people in the park were in a hurry to get home before the storm. They never even noticed the strange creature who brought the wizard's hat back to him. The creature slipped back into the water as soon as the hat was on Harrison Peabody's head. Little rivers of water trickled down from the hat. The wizard was too excited to care. "George!" he said. "It's been a long time."

The creature poked its head out of the murky water. "It's been years, Peabody," the husky voice said, "but you haven't changed much."

Rick and Barbara were down on their hands and knees on the stone wall. They leaned over the water and tried to get a better view of the creature.

"It has a body like a snake," Rick whispered.

"Sh-sh," Barbara said.

By now there were no other people in the park. Harrison Peabody looked down at the two children kneeling beside him. "Barbara, Rick," he said, "I want you to meet an old friend of mine. This is George."

"How do you do?" Barbara said.

"Pleased to meet you," the creature answered.

"What is he?" Rick asked.

At this George reared up into the air. He twisted his body so that long, scaly curves of what looked like a giant fire hose looped out of the water.

"He's showing you what he is," the wizard said. "A sea serpent."

"Aren't you a bit mixed-up, George?"

Rick said. "This isn't the sea. It's a lake."

"I'll have you know," the serpent said, "that Brooklyn has had sea serpents for a long time." He glared at Rick.

The wizard said, "Remember that time — a long time ago — John Van Nyse claimed he saw five great sea serpents rise out of Steinbokkery Pond?"

George laughed so hard that his whole long body shook. It churned up the lake in white foam. "I could understand if he said four. My brother Pete and I were playing in the moonlight. Van Nyse could have seen our reflections in the pond. But *five*? He must have been drunk."

"He said there were flames bursting from your head," Harrison Peabody reminded him.

"Phosphorus," the serpent said. "I glow in the dark."

"Like a firefly?" Barbara asked.

The serpent nodded.

"I never even heard of Stein-whatever-it-is Pond," Rick said. "Where is it?"

"Not too far from here," the wizard told him. "On the other side of this park, I should say."

The serpent shook his head. "Not any more, Peabody," he said. "They drained the pond and put the old Lefferts house in its place. That's why I came here." He looked at the broken bottles and tin cans in the lake. "Steinbokkery Pond was much nicer." The serpent gave a gusty sigh. His long, scaly body quivered in the murky water.

"Let bygones be bygones," Harrison Peabody said. "What about giving my friends a ride, George?"

The serpent's mouth stretched into a smile. He looked like a good-natured alligator. "That sounds like fun," he said. "Just tell them to hold tight. I don't want them falling into this dirty water."

15

THE serpent arched his back. A long loop of him curved up out of the water. The wizard pointed to it. "Climb aboard." He stepped off the stone wall onto George's back. Harrison Peabody hugged the serpent with one arm. In the other hand he held his umbrella.

Rick was next. He crawled behind the wizard and grabbed the scaly body of the serpent with both hands.

Barbara expected the serpent's back to be slimy and slippery. But the scales were dry and hard. She seated herself behind Rick and put her arms around his waist.

"Ready?" Harrison Peabody asked.

"Yes," Rick and Barbara said together.

The serpent glided forward. His head went in and out of the water. But he kept the big curve of his back high and dry. His tail splashed behind them like a propeller.

They whizzed around the lake. Barbara was enjoying the ride. Suddenly she felt a drop of water on her nose. Then another. In a minute it was raining hard.

Harrison Peabody sat up straight and locked his legs around the serpent. He opened his umbrella. "Please," he said to the umbrella, "keep the rain off all three of us."

The umbrella didn't get any bigger, but Rick and Barbara found that even though the rain was falling all around them they weren't getting wet.

Rick was sure the umbrella could do more interesting things than just keep the rain off. He wondered if it would listen to him. He looked at the lake below. All at once he had an idea. "Please, magic umbrella," he said, "make the air warm and the water clean."

It was still raining hard, but Rick and Barbara suddenly felt much too hot in their jackets. The lake looked cool and inviting.

"We'd like to be in bathing suits," Barbara said.

Nothing happened.

"Please," she added.

Rick found that he was wearing a pair of blue swim trunks. Barbara had on a yellow bathing suit. And Harrison Peabody was dressed in an old-fashioned, two-piece, striped bathing suit. It was like the ones in the silent movies Mrs. Cunningham liked to watch on television. The wizard didn't seem to think there was anything unusual about his suit.

"Last one in is a rotten egg." Barbara dived into the water. Rick jumped in after her, but the wizard stayed where he was. He sat on the serpent's back and held the umbrella over his head.

The two children splashed about in the lake. The rain was pouring all around them, but they couldn't feel it. They could feel the sparkling clear water of the lake.

Barbara swam underwater and chased a sunfish. Then she rolled over onto her back and looked at the rain drops that never quite reached her.

"I'll race you to the island." Rick began to swim toward a little island that was

covered with trees. Barbara turned over onto her stomach and swam after him.

Barbara caught up with Rick before he reached the long brown grass that grew out of the water at the edge of the island. Her knees touched the sandy bottom of the lake. Barbara stood up. She brushed her hair out of her eyes and looked at the sky. It wasn't so dark now. And the rain was just a drizzle.

A moment later a bright shaft of sunlight came through the clouds. The rain stopped.

16

HARRISON PEABODY closed his umbrella and tucked it under his arm. "An April shower," he said.

The air was still warm, and the water was clean. It was even more fun to swim when the sun was shining.

"Why don't you come in the water, Harry?" Rick called.

The little man blushed and didn't answer.

George slid through the water toward the children. "Peabody can't swim," he told them in his husky voice. The serpent turned to look at the lake shore. Now that the sun was out, people were coming back into the park.

"Hold your breath, Peabody. And hang on! We're going under." The serpent dived down into the water.

Rick and Barbara saw Harrison Peabody carried down into the lake. A line of foam told them that the serpent was swimming toward the shore. They swam after him as fast as they could.

George took the little wizard to the edge of the lake. He left him in the shallow water near the stone wall. Then the serpent sank under the surface of the water, and the children couldn't see him any more.

Harrison Peabody was coughing and sputtering. Rick and Barbara helped him to climb out of the lake.

A crowd of curious people began to gather near them. Barbara heard a man say, "If a policeman sees them, they'll be locked up. It's against the law to swim in that lake."

"It's hotter than I ever remember for this time of year," a woman said. "But that doesn't mean you can run around like *that!*"

A police car was driving slowly along the road through the park. When the two policemen in it saw the crowd of people they stopped the car. Rick and Barbara grabbed Harrison Peabody by the hands. They pulled him toward the gate of the park. When they saw one of the policemen get out of the police car the children began to run. The wizard puffed along between them. They didn't stop running until they reached the front porch of the Benton house.

"Oh!" Harrison Peabody gasped. "I dropped my umbrella in the lake!"

"And I don't have my door key any more," Barbara said. "It was in the pocket of the jacket I was wearing. There's no pocket in this bathing suit."

Barbara didn't want to ring the doorbell. She would never be able to explain
to Mrs. Cunningham why they were
wearing bathing suits.

Rick climbed onto the porch railing.
He shinnied up the pole in the corner
and swung himself up onto the roof of
the porch. Barbara had left her bedroom
window open. Rick slipped through it

and tiptoed downstairs to open the front door for his sister and the wizard.

Mrs. Cunningham heard him open the door. She was in the kitchen getting supper ready. "Is that you, children?" she called. "Did you get caught in the rain?"

"Yes," Barbara answered. "We're going upstairs to change."

The two children and the wizard raced up the stairs. Rick got the stepladder from his room and helped Harrison Peabody up into the attic. Before he closed the trapdoor the little man looked down and said, "I don't have anything to change into."

"What happened to your other suit?" Rick asked.

"I turned it into the new one," the wizard said in a sad little voice. Then he brightened. "Oh, yes, I do have the socks and underwear Barbara dried for me."

17

Mrs. Cunningham made beef stew for supper. Barbara was able to shovel quite a lot of it into a plastic bag. After supper the children took it upstairs to the wizard.

Rick tapped on the trapdoor with the broom handle. Harrison Peabody lowered the rope for Rick and Barbara to climb into the attic.

The little man had taken off the wet bathing suit and hung it over the back of one of the chairs to dry. He was wearing his undershirt and shorts and the old black socks.

Barbara noticed that the wizard's eyes

were red. She wondered if he had been crying. His nose was red too.

"Ah-choo!" Harrison Peabody sneezed. "I wish I had a handkerchief."

"I'll get you some Kleenex." Barbara opened the trapdoor. She heard the roar of the MGM lion and the sound of music from the television set in the living room. Mrs. Cunningham had settled down to watch *Naughty Marietta*.

Barbara climbed down the rope ladder. She took the box of Kleenex from her room and two blankets from the linen closet in the bathroom. "Rick," she called, "give me a hand with this stuff."

Rick came down from the attic. He got the stepladder out of his room. It made it easier to carry the blankets up to the attic. There wasn't another spare pillow in the linen closet. Barbara took the pillow off her own bed and handed it up through the trapdoor to the wizard.

"Harry's got an awful cold," Rick told her. He went to his father's closet and found a threadbare blue bathrobe. Mr. Benton was very fond of it, but Mrs. Benton wouldn't let him take it along when they went for a trip. Rick put away the stepladder and then climbed the rope ladder with the blue bathrobe under his arm.

"You can wear this for now, Harry," Rick said. "But whatever you do, don't turn it into anything else."

"How can I?" the wizard said. "I don't have my umbrella."

Harrison Peabody put on the bathrobe. It was much too long for him. Barbara rolled up the sleeves so the little man could eat his supper. Rick had remembered to bring a spoon. The wizard ate the stew right out of the plastic bag.

Barbara made up a bed on the rug with the two blankets and the pillow. "Don't worry, Harry," she said. "Tomorrow Rick and I will go to the park and get your umbrella for you. You ought to stay in bed anyway and take care of that cold."

18

On Sunday morning Barbara woke very early. She could hear the rattle of rain on her window pane. She threw off her covers and got up. Her slippers were on the floor beside the bed. Barbara put them on and wiggled into her bathrobe. Then she ran down the hall to Rick's room.

Rick was fast asleep, rolled up in the quilt on his bed. A tuft of his hair stuck out of one end of the quilt, and his bare feet were poking out of the other end.

Barbara tickled the sole of one of Rick's feet. He grunted and turned over onto his stomach.

Barbara tickled his other foot. "Rick, get up. It's raining!"

Rick sat up in bed and rubbed his eyes.

Mrs. Cunningham was still asleep. She had stayed up late the night before. Barbara made oatmeal for breakfast. Then Rick stood guard in front of Mrs. Cunningham's door while Barbara took a glass of orange juice and a bowl of the hot cereal to the wizard.

Barbara used the stepladder to get into the attic. She didn't want to bang on the trapdoor. Harrison Peabody was lying in the makeshift bed Barbara had made on the pretty fringed rug. The little man was snoring softly. Barbara shook him. The wizard opened his eyes.

"How do you feel, Harry?" Barbara asked.

"Terrible," he said. "My head is all stuffed up."

Barbara put the orange juice and the oatmeal on the floor beside the little man's pillow. "Here's your breakfast. Rick and I are going to the park to get your umbrella. Please stay in the attic while we're away. And be careful."

Harrison Peabody looked at the rain trickling down the attic window. "You be careful," he said.

19

THE two children put on their raincoats and rubbers. Barbara left a note on
the kitchen table.

> Dear Mrs. Cunningham,
>   Rick and I lost something
> yesterday. We are going to the
> park to look for it.
>
>   Yours truly,
>   Barbara

On the way to the park Rick and
Barbara found that they were much too
warm in their raincoats.

"It's your fault, Rick," Barbara said.
"You asked the umbrella to make the air
warm."

"But you were the one who changed our jackets and blue jeans into bathing suits," Rick reminded her.

"Now I see," his sister said, "why magic in stories always goes wrong."

"You mean like having three wishes and wishing for all the wrong things?" Rick asked.

"Yes. We ought to make a list of exactly what we want the umbrella to do," Barbara said. "Harry always makes such a mess with his magic. I'm sure we can do better."

They went through the gate of the park and crossed the road. There was no traffic. Cars were not allowed to drive through the park on weekends.

When they reached the stone wall at the edge of the lake they saw that people had already started throwing things into the water. Barbara saw four metal rings from flip-top cans, a piece of plastic with six holes in it to hold the cans, and a section of Saturday's newspaper.

The rain was coming down in a steady drizzle. There were no other people in the park. The children stood on the stone wall and looked out over the lake.

Rick put both hands to his mouth. "George!" he yelled as loud as he could.

Far out in the middle of the lake there was a splash. The water churned into a line of foam. The sea serpent was

swimming toward them. His head stuck out of the water.

George swam close to the stone wall. "Where's Peabody?" he asked in his husky voice.

"He's in bed with a bad cold," Barbara told the serpent. "And anyway, all he has to wear is that funny-looking bathing suit. He needs the umbrella to get his clothes back."

"If you ask me," the sea serpent said, "Peabody would be a lot better off without that fool umbrella."

"He sure would," Rick agreed. "But right now *we* need the umbrella to get our jackets. Barb left our front door key in the pocket of hers."

"Please, George," Barbara begged. "Try to find the umbrella for us."

"Well," the serpent said, looking at her with bright green eyes, "I owe you two something for cleaning up the lake. I only wish it would stay clean." The serpent scooped a sheet of wet newspaper out of the water with his mouth. He laid it on top of the stone wall. Then George swung around. "Just wait here." He dived down into the lake. The water frothed and steamed where he had been a moment before.

Rick and Barbara waited for what seemed a very long time. Suddenly the serpent popped out of the water. He tossed a beer can off his head. Rick caught it.

George was carrying the black umbrella in his mouth. He reared up and laid it on the stone wall beside the children. "I had a hard time finding it," he said. "It was stuck in the mud over by the island."

20

Barbara picked up the umbrella and opened it carefully. It was muddy. One spoke was bent. Otherwise it seemed to be all right.

"Don't forget," George said, "that's *Peabody's* umbrella."

The sea serpent swung his long body around in a huge arc. He did a double somersault in the air and streaked away from them across the lake. He left in such a hurry that Rick and Barbara never had a chance to thank him for finding the umbrella. They could see him far out in the middle of the lake, rolling and twisting and chasing his tail.

Rick put the beer can in a litter basket. "Come on, Barb," he said. "Work the magic."

Barbara had done a lot of thinking while the serpent was looking for the umbrella. She held the umbrella over her head now and looked up at it. "Pretty please, dear Umbrella," she said, "change all three of those bathing suits back to the clothes that they were before. And make the air the way it ought to be in April." The umbrella gave a little jerk and almost pulled itself out of Barbara's grasp.

Rick reached up and grabbed the umbrella with both hands. Barbara let go of it. "While you're at it, Umbrella," Rick said, "how about taking Barb and me to the zoo?"

Nothing happened.

Rick looked at the umbrella. "Oh, all right," he said. "Please, please, please!"

The umbrella began to rise in the air. "Oops!" Rick said.

Barbara caught hold of Rick's ankles before he was yanked away. The two children were pulled higher and higher. The umbrella sailed just over the treetops. Some of the trees were covered with little red buds. And some had leaves already out. The umbrella swooped up and down as if it were playing a game. When Barbara reached out to touch a magnolia blossom, she almost lost her grip on Rick's ankle.

The umbrella bobbed over the iron fence around the zoo. It came down just outside the elephant's cage. The elephant was using his trunk to pick up wet straw. He raised his head to look at the children standing under the black umbrella. Then he snorted and tossed the straw onto his back.

"It's a shame that the elephant has to be shut up in a cage with nothing to do all day," Barbara said. "And the park is so great at this time of the year."

Rick had an idea. "He doesn't have to be shut up." Rick looked up at the umbrella. "Please let the zoo animals go free in the park."

Suddenly the elephant was gone from his cage. A happy trumpeting came from outside the tall iron fence of the zoo. Rick and Barbara heard the roar of a lion on Lookout Mountain.

Barbara knew she had to do something. She was sorry for the animals in the cages, but it wasn't safe to have them running around loose. Barbara grabbed the umbrella away from Rick. But she was too late.

It had stopped raining.

21

Rɪᴄᴋ and Barbara heard excited voices. Then there was the sound of running feet. Two zoo keepers ran past them. They were carrying nets. "Which way did the tiger go?" one keeper yelled to the other.

The men raced up the steps and out of the big gate of the zoo. They tore off down the road that led through the park.

Barbara closed the umbrella. She and Rick left the zoo. They began to walk through the woods. Now they could hear sirens. Two police cars went shrieking down the road.

A deer with a little spotted fawn leaped across the path in front of the children. Two zebras were playing in the Long Meadow. Overhead an eagle swooped.

"Hey, Barb, look!" Rick pointed to an enormous beech tree. Barbara saw a little monkey with a long tail chasing a gray squirrel. The squirrel had never seen a monkey before. He chattered in fright and climbed higher and higher in the tree.

Now that the rain had stopped, people were coming into the park. Mothers pushed baby carriages along the walks. People of all ages rode bicycles on the roadway.

Rick and Barbara joined a crowd on the lake shore. "Somebody saw an alligator in the lake," a boy with a fishing pole told Rick.

A women screamed, "There it is!"

"What's that next to it?" a man asked. "It looks like a hippopotamus."

Three police cars and a large green van drove up close to the lake. The policemen got out of their cars. They ordered the people to move back from the water's edge.

"Just keep calm, everybody," one policeman said. "Lady, is that your little boy? Hold onto him. Alligators move fast."

There were two zoo men in the van. They both carried ropes and heavy nets. The policemen cleared a path for them through the crowd. The zoo men walked to the lake shore. One of them whistled. He held out a piece of meat.

"Here, Jenny," the zoo man called.

A fat old alligator waddled out of the water. The zoo man waved the meat and backed away.

"Good girl, Jenny," he said.

As soon as the alligator was clear of the water the keeper threw the meat to her. The other zoo man tossed a thick net over her. The alligator thrashed her tail and struggled, but she was caught. The two keepers lifted the alligator into the van.

When the zoo men tried to catch the hippo, he swam to the middle of the lake and played submarine. "We'll have to use a dragnet," a policeman said. "Who wants to help?"

Almost everybody did. They spread a big net along one side of the lake and slowly dragged it to the other side. It wasn't just the hippo they caught in the net. There were sea lions, a beaver, a pair of otters, and a lot of fish in the net when it was pulled out of the lake. The people scooped up the fish and threw them back into the water.

Something else was in the net — all curled up into a very large ball of silvery green scales. Nobody seemed to know what it was. Rick and Barbara stared at it.

"It's George!" Barbara whispered. "They've caught George!"

22

THE zoo men were looking at the sea serpent. Barbara and Rick heard one of the men say, "Wow! Look at the size of this guy! I wonder what he is. Whatever he is, he didn't come from the zoo. And we don't have room for him there."

"We could put him in the alligator pen with old Jenny," the other man said.

"We can't risk it. They might fight. I'd hate to have anything happen to Jenny. We don't know anything about this fellow. Anyway, we can't leave him here."

The men threw a net over George and hoisted him into the green van. Then they drove away down the road.

The children watched until the van was out of sight. Barbara said, "We'd better go. We have to take Harry his lunch."

Rick and Barbara walked home in silence. Both of them remembered the sea serpent doing somersaults and chasing his tail in the lake. He couldn't do that in a pen. They felt much too bad about what had happened to George to talk.

Mrs. Cunningham opened the front door when Barbara rang the bell. "Did you find what you were looking for?" she asked.

"Yes," Barbara told her.

Mrs. Cunningham took the children's raincoats and hung them in the hall closet. While Rick and Barbara were pulling off their rubbers, Mrs. Cunningham picked up the umbrella and put it away in the closet too.

"Hurry and get your lunch, children. It turned out to be a nice day after all. I thought I'd take you to Coney Island this afternoon." Mrs. Cunningham looked excited. "I haven't been to Coney Island for years," she said.

After lunch Barbara cleared the table. While Mrs. Cunningham was loading the dishwasher, Barbara dumped the leftover tunafish salad into a plastic bag. She gave it to Rick. "Don't forget to take Harry his umbrella. It's in the hall closet," she whispered.

Rick tucked the plastic bag under his shirt front and went to the closet for the umbrella. Then he ran upstairs and banged with the broom on the trapdoor of the attic.

The trapdoor opened. Harrison Peabody peeped out. When he saw Rick he let down the rope ladder. Rick climbed

up. He handed the wizard the umbrella he was carrying.

The little man was once more dressed in his checked suit. He smiled. "I knew you got the umbrella back when my bathing suit turned into this," he said. "I suppose George found the umbrella for you?"

Rick nodded.

"Good old George!" the wizard said.

Rick couldn't bear to tell Harrison Peabody what had happened. He knew it was all his fault. He pulled the bag of tunafish salad out from under his shirt. "Here's your lunch, Harry. I have to go now. Mrs. Cunningham is taking Barb and me to Coney Island. We'll see you when we get back."

Rick backed out of the attic and climbed down the rope ladder. The wizard pulled up the ladder and closed the trapdoor.

23

MRS. CUNNINGHAM and the children walked down Albemarle Road to the subway station.

Barbara and Rick were wearing their jackets. Rick had found his in the drawer where he had stuffed the wet bathing suit the day before. His shoes and jeans and underwear were all crammed in with the jacket. Rick had a hard time opening the drawer.

Barbara had no problem. Her clothes were all in her closet where she had hung the dripping suit. The front door key was safe in the pocket of her jacket.

Most of the way the train ran on elevated tracks high above the ground. The children looked out over the roofs of Brooklyn. When the train came near Coney Island they saw the boardwalk and the huge ferris wheel.

"Look, children!" Mrs. Cunningham pointed.

Between two tall apartment buildings Rick and Barbara caught a glimpse of the shining sea.

The train came to the end of the line. Everybody got off. Rick, Barbara, and Mrs. Cunningham walked along a wooden platform and down a stairway to the street.

Barbara wanted to ride the roller coaster. Rick said it made him sick.

"It makes me sick too," Mrs. Cunningham said.

They walked along the boardwalk to the pier. People were fishing there. Rick

watched a funny blowfish puff itself up like a balloon. Barbara and Mrs. Cunningham were happy when the man who caught the blowfish threw it back into the water.

"If you want to see interesting fish," the man said, "you ought to go to the aquarium."

The aquarium was a long low building. The entrance was on the boardwalk. Once inside they walked down a dark hall past the brightly lit plate-glass windows of large tanks. They stopped to watch an electric eel light up a light bulb. Mrs. Cunningham looked at the octopus while Rick looked at the sharks. And Barbara saw live sea horses for the first time in her life.

Then they all went outdoors to the open deck. A killer whale was splashing around in a tank there. "He's really very friendly," one of the aquarium men told

Rick. The man reached into the tank to pet the whale.

Barbara pointed to a tank with a crowd of people around it. "What's over there?"

"It's a new arrival," the aquarium man said.

Mrs. Cunningham walked over to the crowd. Rick and Barbara joined her.

"What is it?" a man said. "Sure looks funny."

"Well," the woman beside him said, "we can't stand here all day waiting for it to do something. Let's go look at the seals."

The crowd began to thin out. Mrs. Cunningham and the children were able to get to the railing around the tank. They looked down into the water.

Curled up in the bottom of the cement tank was a very large ball of silvery green scales. The ball of scales twitched. Barbara saw the glint of angry green eyes.

It was George!

24

Mrs. Cunningham was soon tired of watching the ball of silvery green scales. "I read in the *Times* this morning that there are some baby whales here at the aquarium," she said. "I'll go look at them. Come and join me when you're through looking at Old Scaly." She walked across the open deck to where a crowd had gathered around the whale tank.

Now only Rick and Barbara were standing beside the railing. George uncoiled himself enough to stick his head out. "Old Scaly indeed!" he hissed. He glared at the children. "Something tells me you two are to blame for the mess I'm in. Well, you ought to be able to get me out of it soon. It's starting to rain." The sea serpent reared his long neck up out of the tank of water. He turned to look at the open sea. "I've had enough of that lake," he said. "You're right, Rick. I belong out there in the ocean. Now use the umbrella to get me there. And watch how you talk to it. The fool thing likes to play tricks."

"I gave the umbrella back to Harry," Rick said.

"And he's home in bed with a bad cold," Barbara told the sea serpent.

"Just my luck!" George glared again at the children and dived to the bottom of his tank.

Now Rick and Barbara felt the rain. It was beginning to come down hard. Mrs. Cunningham came running over to them. "That's how it is with an April day." She smiled. "Lucky I brought an umbrella, even if all I could find was this dirty old thing."

Barbara looked at the muddy black umbrella. Her heart began to pound inside her.

Mrs. Cunningham opened the umbrella and held it over the children. Barbara looked up. She could see the bent spoke.

"Dear, darling, sweet Umbrella," Barbara said, "please put George where he wants to be!"

Barbara heard a husky voice say, "Good girl!"

Then Mrs. Cunningham said, "We'd better go inside out of the rain, children." She looked into the tank. "Well, I see Old Scaly is gone," she said. "They must have found a better place to put him."

25

MRS. CUNNINGHAM took the children
to a restaurant for dinner. Both Rick and
Barbara ordered stuffed cabbage. It was
very late when the three of them got
home. And it was raining hard.

It was time for the Sunday night movie
on television. Mrs. Cunningham sat down
in the living room to watch it. Rick quietly
went to the hall closet. He took out the
black umbrella. Mrs. Cunningham had
put it there when she walked into the
house.

Barbara took the umbrella away from him. She gave it a little hug. Then the two children went upstairs. Rick tapped on the trapdoor with the broom handle.

Harrison Peabody opened the trapdoor. He let down the rope ladder. Rick climbed up first. Barbara came after him with the umbrella. She was still on the ladder when the little man said, "Do you think you could get me some supper, Barbara? I've had nothing since lunchtime. When it began to rain this afternoon I tried to magic up a little something. But my umbrella is in a nasty mood. I can't get it to do anything."

Barbara climbed into the attic. She opened the umbrella and looked up at it. "Dear Umbrella," she said, "please set the table with a dinner Harry will enjoy. And please will you clean up the dirty dishes afterward?"

At once a platter of corned beef and cabbage appeared on the table.

Harrison Peabody stared. Barbara closed the umbrella and handed it to him. "Rick gave you the wrong umbrella by mistake," she said.

The wizard sat down at the table. While he ate his dinner Rick and Barbara told him all the adventures of the day.

The little man listened without interrupting. Then he said, "The trouble with magic is that it's terribly hard to handle." The wizard ate the last bite of cabbage, and the platter vanished. In its place was a dish of chocolate chip ice cream. "Would you like some?" Harrison Peabody asked the children.

Before Rick and Barbara had time to answer, two more dishes of ice cream were on the table. There were two more spoons too.

The wizard rubbed his chin. "I've never known this to happen before," he said. "The umbrella must have taken a liking to you."

When they had finished the ice cream, all the dishes disappeared from the table.

Barbara had been thinking. "Harry," she said, "suppose Daddy and Mother

come home and see the attic like this?"

Rick remembered something. "This is where Dad puts the suitcases when he comes home from a trip."

Harrison Peabody stood up. He walked to the attic window and looked out. It was still raining. "We had fun," Harrison Peabody said. "Didn't we?"

"Oh, yes!" Barbara and Rick said together.

The wizard opened the magic umbrella and held it over his head. "Please," he said, speaking slowly and carefully, "change everything back to the way it was before."

The children looked around the dusty attic filled with cobwebs and old magazines. The little man whispered something to his umbrella. He smiled at Rick and Barbara.

An instant later, both the umbrella and Harrison Peabody were gone.